Mr. Sunnyside
– Imagination! –

gatekeeper press™
Columbus, OH

Mr. Sunnyside: Imagination

Published by Gatekeeper Press
2167 Stringtown Rd, Suite 109
Columbus, OH 43123-2989
www.GatekeeperPress.com

Library of Congress Control Number: 2021936273

ISBN (hardcover): 9781662912580
ISBN (paperback): 9781662912597
eISBN: 9781662912603

My first book is dedicated to my loving wife Barbara, who is also my best editor. I would also like to dedicate this to my kids and grandchildren who, like me, love cartoons.

"Uh-oh! Mommy, it's raining out!"

"Tommy, please stay in your bedroom and play with your toys. I'm in the kitchen getting breakfast ready."

"But Mommy, I want to go outside and ride my new skateboard. I don't like these toys anymore. They're boring!"

"Tommy, you can't go outside. You will get wet and catch a cold. I don't want you to miss any more school days. You were just home sick last week."

"Alright, Mommy! I will try to play with my old boring toys. I wish I had someone to play with."

Whoosh - swish - pop!

"Incoming egg!"

"Who are you?"

"Why, Tommy, I'm Mr. Sunnyside!
I'm here to play with you and brighten up
your day."

"How will you do that? It's raining out, and my mom doesn't want me to go out. I might get sick! I don't want to miss any more school. Today is the beginning of Easter recess."

"Tommy, we are gonna learn about imagination and make your old boring toys come to life."

"Hey, Tommy, did you know toys should be played with?"

"Is that why they call them toys?"

"Eggsactly!"

"What's imagi.........?"

"You'll find out. Let's get crackin!"

"Tommy, who are you talking to?"

"Mommy, it's my new friend,
Mr. Sunnyside!"

"Who? I don't see or hear him."

"Okay, Tommy, it's time for breakfast. Come and have some eggs and toast. I made your eggs just like you like them, sunnyside up!"

"UGHHHH, Mommy, can I have pancakes instead? I don't want to hurt my new friend's feelings. And actually, I'm not hungry right now. We are going to play!"

"Alright, Tommy, but only for an hour. Have fun with your new friend,

Mr. Whatever."

"Mommy, his name is Mr. Sunnyside."

"Okay, Tommy, but in a little while you have to eat! Breakfast is the most important meal of the day and eggs are very nutritious."

"Mommy, can we just save them for Easter, please? Yuck on eggs, I want happy face pancakes with chocolate chips, extra butter, and syrup. They're deeelicious , and yummy to the tummy!"

"Hey, Tommy, look at me go on my skateboard!"

Whoosh, swish and wheee!"

"Wow, Mr. Sunnyside, you look so cool on your skateboard!"

"Tommy, hop on and hold on to me. We're gonna eggscape!

Whoosh, wheee, and we're off!

Isn't this eggciting?"

"Yeah, Mr. Sunnyside, your skateboard is almost like mine!

Can I see more imagi...Mr. Sunnyside?"

"Tommy, you mean imagination. Yes, you can. You can come and float with me, but only for a few seconds. I have to hold my breath till I turn blue, then I have to stop. Are you ready to feel like you're on a balloon?"

"Yeah let's imagi it!"

Alrighty! Hang on! Here we go – up, up and away, wheeee!"

"Gee, Mr. Sunnyside, you look like an Easter egg! Hey, Mr. Sunnyside, why is it I'm the only one who can see you?"

"Well, Tommy, it's because you called upon me. I'm here to help you learn about that word I mentioned before."

"What's that?"

"It's called imagination."

"Imagi – whaaa?!"

"It's what we're doing right now!"

"Mr. Sunnyside, it almost feels like we're outside."

"Tommy, I hope you're having an eggciting time!"

"Now it's time for me to eggxit and catch up with some of my friends, like Scrambaline."

"Mr. Sunnyside, can I meet your friends?"

"Not right now, Tommy. Time for you to eat breakfast. Time for me to eggxit! Poof! Maybe you can meet some of my friends in our next adventure. Till then, have fun playing and remember to use your imagination!"

"Bye, bye, my new friend."
"Bye, Mr. Sunnyside!"

"Wait .....Mr. Sunnyside!"

"Tommy, who are you talking to?"

"No one, Mommy, just using my imagination."

Pop!

Mr. Sunnyside gives a wink to Tommy.

"Tommy, come and get your eggs before they get cold."

Tommy turns to Mr. Sunnyside and shrugs.

Poof!

The End

(for now)

First and foremost, I want to thank Stephanie Richoll for her illustrations to my words. Her work is like beautiful music to ordinary lyrics. She is so gifted and patient. Stephanie had to put up with my email craziness and imagination.

Thanks to my cousin Tom and my egg-shaped head for inspiring me to write this story over thirty years ago.

A very special thanks to author Nora D'Ecclesis for referring me to Tony Chellini and Eden Tuckman at Gatekeeper Press. What a Team!!!

Thanks also to fellow children's author Erin Rafanello Ferguson, who kept telling me that I needed to finish "Mr. Sunnyside." In addition, thanks for support and advice from authors Jessica Valentin, Christine Osoria, and Sandhi Santini. Finally, a special thanks to Catherine Campisi who indirectly hooked me up to the same illustrator who did Jessica's book.

Personal author note:

Our children today, who are gentle like egg shells and vulnerable, need special attention. I hope that this book, and future books that I write, will help them in some way.

CK Gregory, Author, worked in many areas of theatre and the media, both in front and behind the scenes. Now, he is embarking on a new career as a children's author. This is his first book in a series of eggstra adventures to come!

Stephanie Richoll, Illustrator, is a Florida native jack-of-all-trades artist. Now an established illustrator, painter, and graphic designer, she has worked with several publishers and producers and has illustrated several published children's books and novels. She hopes to travel the world, but for now is working with clients all over the world and hopes to continue producing art for amazing projects in the future to come!